Based on a translation by Susan Beard

First published in Swedish as
Lilla syster Kanin blir jagad av en räv
by Bonnier Carlsen Bokförlag
Text © 1987 Ulf Nilsson
Illustrations © 1987 Eva Eriksson
English version © 2017 Floris Books
www.florisbooks.co.uk
British Library CIP Data available
ISBN 978-178250-378-1
Printed in Malaysia

Little Sister Rabbit and the Fox

Ulf Nilsson and Eva Eriksson

Floris
Books

Little Sister Rabbit peeped out of her burrow.
The sun was high in the sky and all the foxes
had gone home to bed.

Now she could hop outside and play.

She squeaked a merry morning song as she bounced off through the warm grass.

Soon she heard the rumbling and growling of an empty tummy, but she couldn't see any other animals around.

There must be something wrong with her ears…

As she hopped along, she tried to whistle like
Big Brother Rabbit had taught her. But no sound
came out – just a rude noise!

So she practised doing somersaults instead.
Then she noticed a nasty smell in the air,
like a hungry fox on the prowl.

There must be something wrong with her nose…

She went to the meadow to pick blue flowers.
But what was that? Did she catch a glimpse of
fiery red fur in a nearby bush?

There must be something wrong with her eyes…

Suddenly, a fox cub who was still awake popped out from the bush. He was a hungry little rascal, poking and sniffing about in the woods, on the lookout for something to catch. Something to eat for dinner.

Little Sister Rabbit dropped the blue flowers and stayed very still.

She was very, very afraid.
The fox cub jumped towards her and barked:
"Yap-yap!"

Little Sister Rabbit stood perfectly still.
The fox cub sniffed her and licked his lips. He was
hungry. He was thinking of rabbit sausages with ketchup.

This fox is going to eat me, she thought. *No one can help me.*
The fox opened his jaws and his teeth glittered like ice.
Little Sister Rabbit didn't try to be brave. She closed her eyes
and thought: *This fox is going to eat me…*

But when the fox cub nipped her she shouted,
"Ow, what are you doing, you naughty beast? Ow!"
She actually got very angry indeed. "Don't bite me,
you silly thing!"
She bounced up in an enormous leap and broke free.

Little Sister Rabbit ran away as fast as she could.
She sprinted around a bush and leaped over a rock.
The fox cub raced after her, barking.

Rabbits are not very brave. They are not born to be brave.
They are born to run and run as fast as their legs can carry them.
So Little Sister Rabbit raced up one hill and down another.
And the fox cub came panting after her.

"Come back! You're mine, little rabbit! Come back right now!"
the hungry fox cub howled, his empty tummy rumbling.

But Little Sister Rabbit kept on running. Her legs scampered,
and her paws pitter-pattered, and the air whistled past her long ears.

One lap around the meadow, two, three… and the fox was so tired from chasing her he had to stop for a sleep. She was going to make it!

Little Sister Rabbit skipped all the way home whistling.

Yes, *whistling*! Now she could do *that* too.

Foxes aren't always dangerous but they *always* have sharp teeth.
Luckily the rabbit family had plenty of sticking plasters at home.